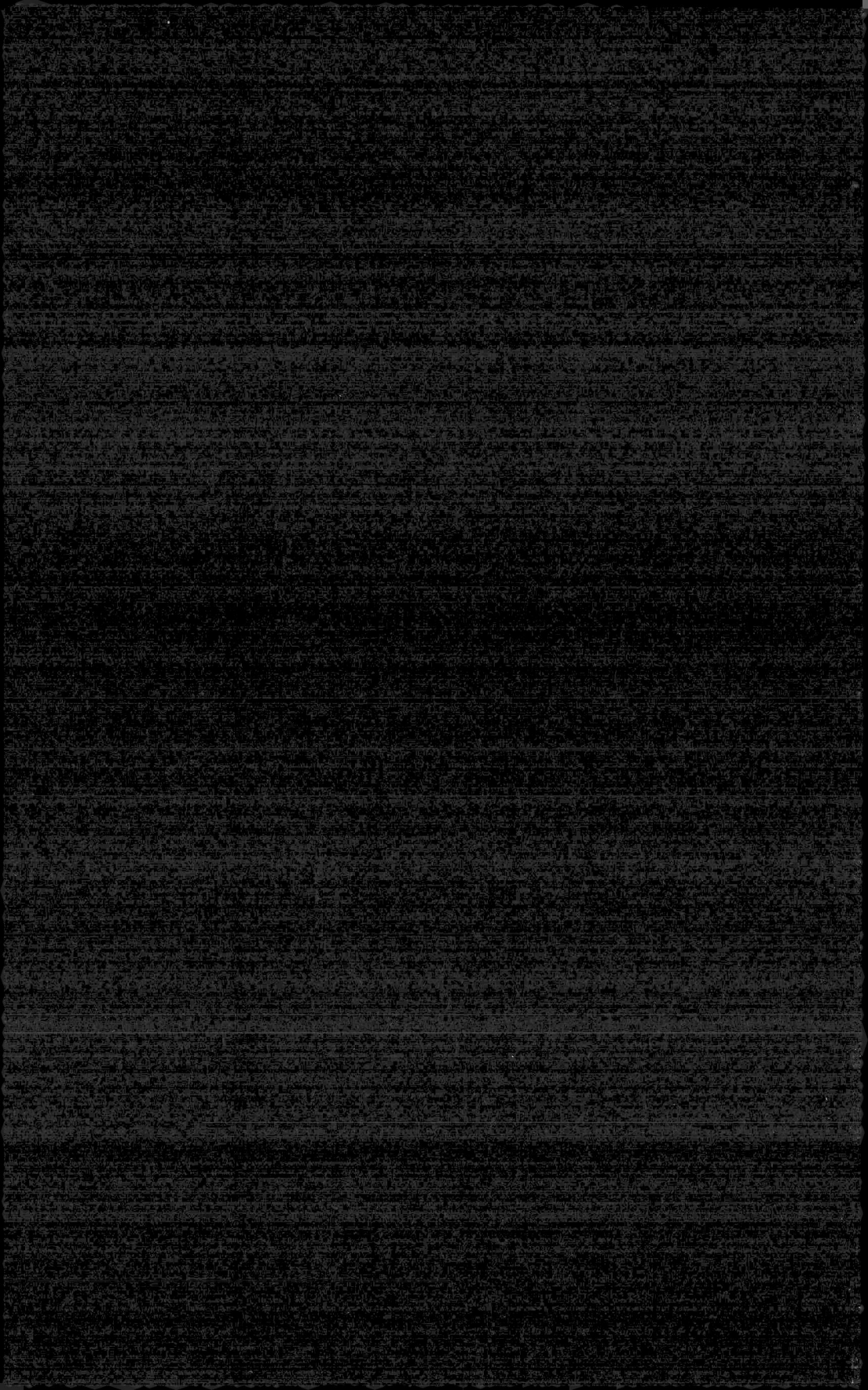

Slightly Salty

Illustrated Poems by
COLIN NEWNHAM

Austin Macauley Publishers™
LONDON · CAMBRIDGE · NEW YORK · SHARJAH

Copyright © Colin Newnham (2017)
The right of Colin Newnham to be identified as author of this work has been asserted by him in accordance with section 77 and 78 of the Copyright, Designs and Patents Act 1988.

All rights reserved. No part of this publication may be reproduced, stored in a retrieval system, or transmitted in any form or by any means, electronic, mechanical, photocopying, recording, or otherwise, without the prior permission of the publishers.

Any person who commits any unauthorized act in relation to this publication may be liable to criminal prosecution and civil claims for damages.

A CIP catalogue record for this title is available from the British Library.

ISBN 978-1-78554-760-7 (Paperback)
ISBN 978-1-78554-761-4 (Hardback)
ISBN 978-1-78554-762-1 (E-Book)

www.austinmacauley.com
First Published (2017)
Austin Macauley Publishers ™ Ltd.
25 Canada Square
Canary Wharf
London
E14 5LQ

Introduction

My interest in writing and painting was dormant until I joined the Ashford Branch of Parkinson's UK who along with many other activities offered painting as a short course under the supervision of a tutor with experience of those with special needs.

I only needed to be asked once and I was soon enrolled.

If a picture paints a thousand words, sang Telly Savalas a long time ago it seemed to me that I could do something for friends and family that would be original and amusing, being tone deaf and having no desire to write song lyrics let alone sing anywhere other than in the proverbial bath tub. I decided to write a poem that spoke up for those, including animals, who were unable to speak for themselves, as well as some that could be generously described as educational and a few that were just downright silly.

You can find out about the Arty Guffles and meet a Drizard, there are some comments by Dolphins and even Rats in space. An All Amphibian Band and a Snail hitchhiking to France will make you smile, Polar Bears and Giraffes, Newts and Gannets can be found and a Pecker Knocker is a creature new to science and makes an interesting adornment to your front door.

To Carol

With love

from

Colin Newah

Poems by Colin Newnham

Giraffe	7
Sea Bear	9
The Dolphin	10
Drizard	11
Great Spotted Woodpecker	12
Green Woodpecker	13
Newts	14
The Afterlife	16
Rats	18
Tortoise	21
Gannet	22
Remember Me	24
The Arty Guffles	26
Uninvited	29
Ice Age	32
Prehistoric	34
Aardvark	36
Stone Age	38
The Sea Bed	40
A King without a Kingdom	44
A Chronicle of Kings and Queens	45
Iron Age	46
The Vikings	48
King Canute	50
Diminutive Denizens	52
A Land Down Under	54
The Wedding Speech	56

A Frog on a Bus	57
A Snail's Travail	58
In the Doctor's Waiting Room	60
Cockroach	62
A Bunch of Thyme	63
Redit Redit Hopit Plop	64
The Man in the Mirror	69
Pigs	70
The Romans	71
The Bastard Duke	72
At Sea	74
Frog Up	76

Giraffe

A browser of a different kind
On the web now springs to mind

But the wildlife film narrator
Is not talking about data

This browser's fame is for his height
He never heard of a mega byte

This gentle creature mostly quiet
Is so tall because his diet

Of the leaves he loves the best
Grow out of reach of all the rest

Some may stare and others laugh
When they see their first giraffe

The tallest creature since the dinosaurs died
 No enemies threaten there's no need to hide

He won't eat you because he only eats leaves
The youngest and sweetest high up in the trees

Others can't reach, their hunger grows stronger
Now wishing their necks were just a bit longer

Three times your height and may be more
His head six metres above the floor

The giraffe evolved with typical caution
His legs and his feet with his neck in proportion

So beware the next time that you see a giraffe
And think he looks funny and are tempted to laugh

He's mostly good tempered and will do you no harm
But if you laugh at him he loses his charm

And like an elephant who will never forget
An offended giraffe is always a threat

When you ask a giraffe be sure to say please
Remember you only come up to his knees

He is the tallest of that we are sure
Only the elephant weighs any more

So don't be fooled, you may think he looks kind
And don't assume that he will not mind

He probably will and he won't mess around
You won't know what hit you as you fall to the ground

Not even the lion, who knows all the tricks
Will be anywhere near a giraffe when she kicks

Sea Bear

The sea bear lives on snow and ice
He must be tough because it's not very nice
In the frozen north where nothing grows
Why he lives there no one knows

With little shelter and less to eat
He's always hungry with cold feet
No shops with fast food on the shelf
He has to hunt to feed himself

So when in the Artic you take care
And hope that you don't meet a bear
He'll see you coming but you won't see him
The colour of snow he blends well in

From his snow cave hidden well
The sea bear he will sense your smell
You may run but you will find
The sea bear won't be far behind

Head for the sea and jump straight in
Forget it, you should see a sea bear swim
Stand and fight him not much fun
He weighs in at half a ton

So if that bear you ever meet
Just pray he's had enough to eat
Because if he's hungry it's for sure
He'll eat you up and look for more

The Dolphin

I am a bottle nose dolphin, I don't have a name
There are thousands of us down here and we all look just the same

We live in the sea which is great but I wish
People would remember that we are not fish

Fish are quite stupid and are caught in big ships
Cooked in hot fat and then eaten with chips

But dolphins are mammals and kings of the seas
Jump out of the water with the greatest of ease

We can talk to each other when we are below
And tell other dolphins the best place to go

We like to see people when they are afloat
And swim on their bows as guide to their boat

And lead them to safety in the lee of the land
Where there are no rocks just soft yellow sand

Drizard

My Dad calls me a drizard, what kind of name is that
He thought I was a dragon, he is a silly chap

Now he and Mum are lizards and I'm a lizard too
We know; that's what they told him when he took me to the zoo

But he wouldn't listen he says he is a wizard
That my Mum is a fairy queen and I'm a dopey drizard

Now I was thinking, if you don't mind and even if you do
It might be fun for just a while if I came and lived with you

I'm an easy pet to live with, quite happy on the floor
Sometimes you might find me up above the door

If you go out, while you are away could take a look upstairs
I might climb up and for a while sit in your best chair

If you leave the fridge door open while a cake you are a cooking
I might nip in and help myself the moment you're not looking

So here I am please let me stay let fairy queens and drizards
Be forgotten because I am a red backed green tree lizard

Just one more thing you ought to know we lizards like new places
Where we can sit and keep quite still and see your puzzled faces

As you look high and you look low and you look everywhere
Till you don't know where else to look there isn't anywhere

So you might think that we have gone and never will be found
But if you look very carefully we'll be somewhere around

Great Spotted Woodpecker

If you go to the country side in the spring time of the year
And if you listen carefully a cupped hand to your ear

You may hear a sound that you have never heard before
A far off drumming clicking noise like an old and rusty door

If you try to find the place where this noise is coming from
You will need a lot of luck because its maker will be gone

To another tree not far away that now begins to groan
The maker of this noise is there looking for a home

He lives up in the trees so high heard but seldom seen
The greater spotted woodpecker, black and white not green

It was the bird that made the noise that sounded like a creak
Yes that was the woodpecker pecking with his beak

In pecker speak it means hey you look up into my tree
I hope that you will come and live up here with me

Green Woodpecker

Bigger than the greater spotted and more often seen
He's not shy and he's quite big and also he's bright green

Another reason why you know when there is one about
Is that his call is not a song more like a shriek or shout

Some say this call sounds like a laugh that of a witch or crone
But he is shouting to his kin that they are not alone

The place that you may see one if you think there's one around
Is on the lawn not in a tree but down there on the ground

It seems like that is where he finds his favourite things to eat
The grubs and worms and creepy things that live beneath your feet

But when he's not eating on your lawn and nowhere to be seen
He'll be in a tree nearby amongst the leaves so green

The place that he prefers to be the place he likes the best
Is up a tree and in a hole that's where he makes his nest

Newts

Newts my tiny amphibious friends
I think it's time that we made amends
For starting a rumour untrue that offends
And retract it for once and for all

As drunk as a lord the old proverb went
Till someone decided their disdain to vent
On you guys the newts erstwhile innocent
Maligned for no reason at all

In all of our books there isn't a clue
Why that dubious status was pinned upon you
A bad reputation that never was due
You just don't deserve it at all

Many a man you could rightly accuse
Of finding a way to make an excuse
To spend too much of his time on the booze
And do himself no good at all

But under a stone with nothing to fear
Is where a newt lives for most of the year
Not in the pub drinking whisky and beer
We don't serve newts here not at all

So it isn't the newt that we should think
Is the creature most likely to quietly slink
Off to the pub and have too much to drink
Hi lives in a pond after all

Newts don't have a voice they can't say a word
But if they did it wouldn't be slurred
So I speak for them to make sure they are heard
As xxxxxx as a newt that's absurd

The Afterlife

Yes there is a life hereafter
Filled with joy and love and laughter

Where all God's creatures stand together
No favour found for fur or feather

This is the land of milk and honey
You can't get in for love nor money

No room for earthly differentials
Here you are judged by your credentials

The hunter with the hunted waits
To enter through the pearly gates

No more contest to survive
Use tooth and claw to stay alive

Those who suffered most on earth
Will be rewarded for their worth

With nothing for those who acted greedy
Spared not a thought for weak and needy

The bully boys have had their day
There is a fairer better way

The meek now get to run the show
And tell the bad guys where to go

Those who once held all the aces
Have no choice but to swap places

With gentle creatures not so pushy
Who didn't have it quite so cushy

Even if it was dead certain
That you faced the final curtain

With all the rest who told you so
Who would be the first to go

Might you recall the times you had
Were they really all that bad

Would you go or would you say
After you I think I'll stay

Rats

Who would choose to be a rat
Nobody we are sure of that

We come last no grace or favour
We live our lives in constant danger

Never seen when the sun is out
Night time that's when we're about

In the darkness out of sight
Out of trouble we're alright

The rat man plies his beastly trade
He don't scare us we're not afraid

Despite his poisons traps and cats
We won't die because we are rats

If we are hungry is it a sin
To look for food in someone's bin

Or in the rubbish on the street
We only get your waste to eat

But people scream and call us vermin
Put down poisons to exterminate us

Never mind the pain and suffering
When you have eaten too much warfarin

We don't matter better dead
Not a good word ever said

We'd like to live in nice clean places
But we are rats daren't show our faces

No one loves us they won't share
No room for rats not anywhere
If we were pink with nice white teeth
We'd live as pets on Hampstead Heath

But we are rats and not so nice
We spread diseases germs and lice

But they're not ours they come from you
Probably flushed them down your loo

To where we live and hang around
In the sewers under ground

We wouldn't choose to live down drains
To suffer floods each time it rains

The only place where we can roam
Reluctantly we call it home

Of our rights no one thinks twice
Because we are rats and just not nice

Yet when a drug you need to test
A volunteer would be the best

But all those asked said us do that
You always used to use a rat

Before man went up into space
A rat was sent to win the race

His journey home it never started
The ratstronaut from life departed

Much maligned and oft abused
We dirty rats in labs are used

Our lives are lost to test our brains
Most of us prefer the drains.

Tortoise

Famous for winning a race with a hare
Against the odds but he didn't care

It wasn't his race so he didn't mind
Who was first to cross over the line

That was a contest way back in the past
When to be any good you had to be fast

That was the race that went down in history
But for the wrong reason and that is the mystery

Why the race was a measure of fastest and strongest
When what matters most is who goes for longest

The average hare lives a decade or two
A blink of an eye for a tortoise who

If given the time and a diet just right
Would outlive us all clear out of sight

Turtles and terrapins eat meat and grow stronger
But tortoises graze and live for much longer

The story is told that Captain James Cook
On a visit to Tonga a tortoise he took

As a gift to the queen where in complete safety
It lived in the palace till one hundred and eighty

Tortoises many have lived their lives slow
They have no need to hurry they've nowhere to go

So don't be a hare and live your life fast
Be a tortoise live longest come last

Gannet

Our largest sea bird seldom seen
He lives at sea a true marine

If to see one is your wish
You'll only find them where there's fish

Miles from land way out at sea
That's where he lives that's where he'll be

His wings when open to full span
Exceed the height of many a man

From a distance when in flight
Looks like a seagull mostly white

Till he comes a little nearer
When his beauty is much clearer

Only glimpsed when flying high
He'll have to come down from the sky

Then you will see him close and true
His head bright yellow and eye sky blue

At first sight when close he passes
You may think he's wearing glasses

But his sight is better than the rest
At catching fish he is the best

He flies up high he can see deeper
His dive more deadly faster steeper

Beneath the surface unaware
That the gannet was even there

The mackerel a swimmer never beaten
By the gannet will soon be eaten

For those of you who have a boat
Or get the chance to go afloat

And share the gannets company
I'm sure that you'll with me agree

Magnificent is the only word
To describe our super bird

Remember Me

For all my life since I was young till I was let me see
I never had to write things down I used my memory

No need to have a pencil a diary or a pen
In my head I always knew with who and where and when

Then one day I lost it but where I just forget
I'm always trying to find it but without success as yet

Then I think it has returned when something comes to mind
That only half an hour ago I simply couldn't find

I feel there's something missing I'm the victim of a theft
Truth is that it's upped and gone just packed it's bag and left

How would I cope without it and know what I must do
If I don't know I'll have a go expect I'll muddle through

Another thing I've noticed more than coincidental
I can't hear everything you say if you speak soft and gentle

So I've got myself a hearing aid and when someone is talking
I know how to make it squeak just like it isn't working

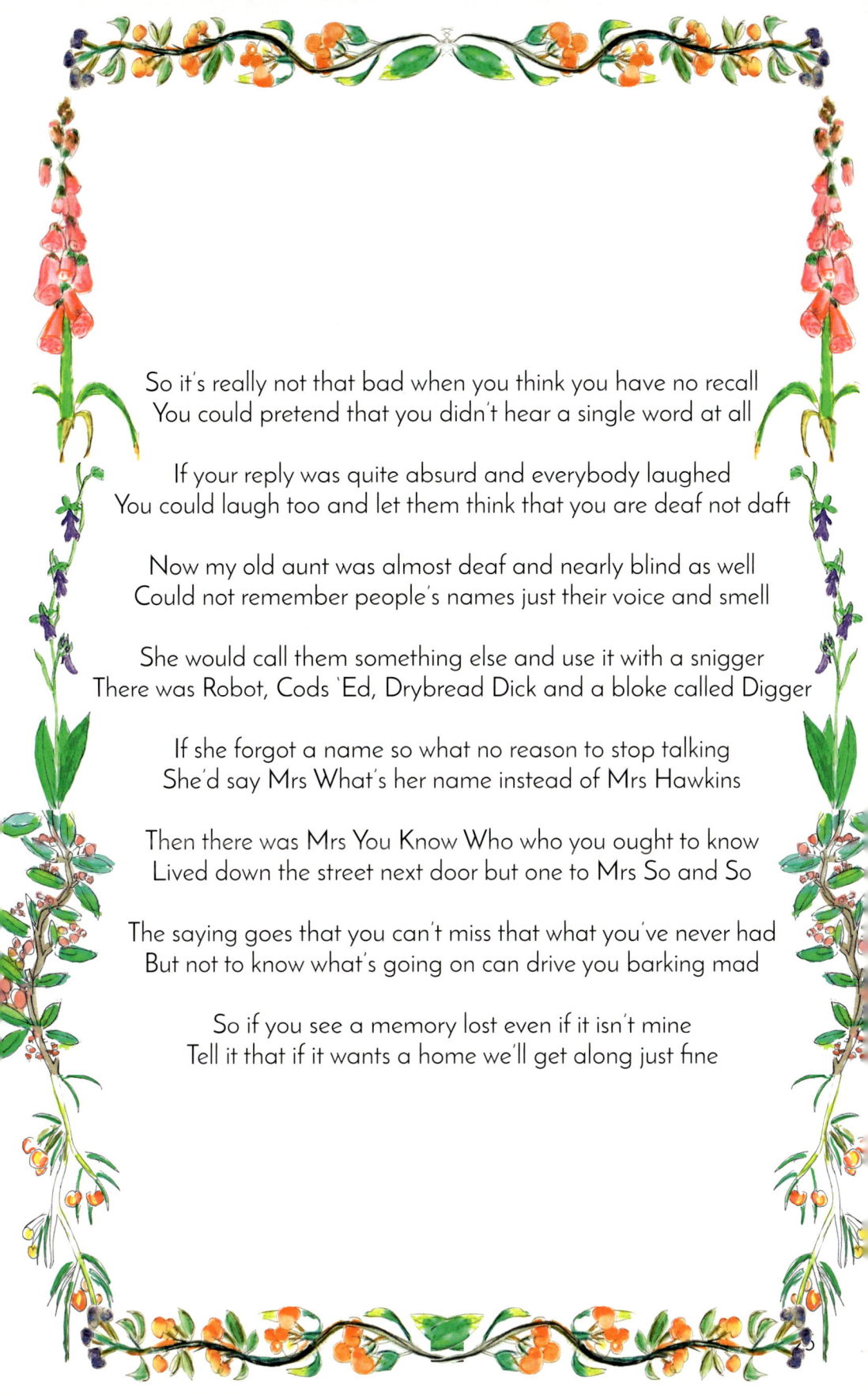

So it's really not that bad when you think you have no recall
You could pretend that you didn't hear a single word at all

If your reply was quite absurd and everybody laughed
You could laugh too and let them think that you are deaf not daft

Now my old aunt was almost deaf and nearly blind as well
Could not remember people's names just their voice and smell

She would call them something else and use it with a snigger
There was Robot, Cods 'Ed, Drybread Dick and a bloke called Digger

If she forgot a name so what no reason to stop talking
She'd say Mrs What's her name instead of Mrs Hawkins

Then there was Mrs You Know Who who you ought to know
Lived down the street next door but one to Mrs So and So

The saying goes that you can't miss that what you've never had
But not to know what's going on can drive you barking mad

So if you see a memory lost even if it isn't mine
Tell it that if it wants a home we'll get along just fine

The Arty Guffles

Some know it all people who've never heard
Say that there is no such word
They've never had the arty guffles

Few have suffered it is quite rare
Once you've had it you'll take care
To avoid the arty guffles

It's not an illness but it is contagious
Makes you do things quite outrageous
Beware of the arty guffles

Suppose one day you chance to meet
A man with quite enormous feet
You might get the arty guffles

Or a lady with a dirty nose
No one tells her but they all knows
That is when you get the arty guffles

You may think that you are super cool
Never felt you were a fool
You will with the arty guffles

First time I thought don't give a toss
Let us see who is the boss
Me or the arty guffles

A funny feeling from within
Told me it would soon begin
The dreaded arty guffles

I tried to talk but could only snigger
I knew my problems would get bigger
If it was the arty guffles

My legs a tremble growing weak
I find that I can hardly speak
Feels like the arty guffles

Then it happened I don't know why
My tongue curled up and my mouth got dry
Looks like the arty guffles

I try to speak can't say a word
I really must look quite absurd
I've got the arty guffles

I must sit down can stand no longer
Deep inside me growing stronger
Lurks the arty guffles

Can't get up weak at the knees
I think that I am going to sneeze
Can't stop the arty guffles

Then someone said here drink some water
I really thought I shouldn't oughta
But I had the arty guffles

In trouble now could hardly breathe
But didn't have the strength to leave
You can't with the arty guffles

Fell off my chair rolled on the floor
I thought I couldn't take much more
Please go now arty guffles

I laughed so much it made me cry
I thought that I might even die
It's tough with the arty guffles

It really couldn't get much worse
I thought that I was going to burst
You don't want the arty guffles

Then it happened quick as lightning
Sneezed so hard it was quite frightening
Out went the arty guffles

Well that's better did the trick
Don't feel dizzy don't feel sick
Ain't got the arty guffles

Next time I thought won't be so silly
Then I met a man called Mr Willey
Not again please not the arty guffles

Uninvited

I met a man the other day
He told me I should go away
And get to know what to expect
I acted somewhat circumspect

I'll introduce you if you like
Felt like saying on yer bike
Decided I should be polite
Not offend or offer slight

Learn about him and his manner
Don't let him put his rusty spanner
In your works so well maintained
Lest his habit be sustained

Seems he's going to live with me
I hope he likes bad company
Seems that I have little choice
No-one there to hear my voice

I'd only known him just a while
But I didn't like his smile
Pushy sort acted clever
Didn't trust him then nor ever

Been some time now since we met
Not a moment to forget
Been there all the bloody time
His agenda never mine

Feel a tremble or a shake
This isn't me it's a mistake
Not so bad when I'm resting
Under pressure can be quite testing

Don't go out much any more
Why can't I get through that door
Want to go but he says no
He'll decide just when we go

Sometimes we stop in a crowd
I feel like calling out aloud
I used to be like you yes you
Did all the things that you can do

Till I met this rotten sod
Thinks he has the power of God
Of us two he is the stronger
I feel that I'm in charge no longer

Lost my balance the other day
I wish that he would go away
Fell to the ground makes me sick
Now I have to use a stick

Took my sense of smell away
Taste went with it on that day
Can't walk straight no I'm not fooling
Never thought that I'd be drooling

So it seems he's here to stay
Shows not a sign he'll go away
And give me back my stolen senses
Taken under false pretences

Optimistic that was me
He won't beat me just you see
That was many years ago
Not beaten yet but pretty slow

Dr Munro said he would
His advice as ever good
Not rule out an operation
To provide amelioration

He knew where they had the knowledge
He referred me to Kings College
They had surgeons with the skills
To operate and ease my ills

Professor Ashkan drilled my head
Said that that should do it
Well Professor that was tough
But we made it through it

Two holes he drilled with consummate care
Right through my skull he knew just where
Would he find his hiding place
Make uninvited show his face

Electrodes battery and a length of cable
Forgotten skills to re-enable
With tablets too 16 each day
We keep him just about at bay

Dr Samuel knows what's right
He gives me what I need to fight
In the long term he may win
Meanwhile I will not give in

DBS has roughed him up
For the moment we aren't speaking
Can this be the turning point
That we are all seeking

Ice Age

The cold of winter could still be felt
The ice stood still refused to melt

It should be summer plants should grow
It didn't rain it fell as snow

In living memory the elders told
Of days when it was not so cold

Grass a plenty for game to eat
Everyone had their daily meat

Now it was too cold to live
Nature frozen nothing to give

A wall of ice came ever south
They had to live from hand to mouth

The sea that you now find at Dover
And need a ferry to cross over

Was freezing more and more each year
The way to leave would soon be clear

The smaller creatures were first to go
They could walk on frozen snow

The woolly mammoth no creature stronger
Was too heavy had to wait longer

With scavengers and vultures hanging round
Till hunger brought its victims down

The frozen sea had made the way
For all to leave no need to stay

And for 20 thousand years or more
Life was absent from our shores

Till the ice released its grip
And we became a living ship

Of creatures who came two by two
The ancestors of me and you

Prehistoric

Prehistoric so we say because we just don't know
What was going on round here a long time ago

Piltdown man surprised us all emerging from the ground
Experts got excited and came from miles around

To see remains of a human skull in a little casket
That raised so many questions if only we could ask it

It took them 40 years to prove that a couple of blokes
Made fools of them with a paleo anthropological hoax

The bones were in fact quite recent not what they claimed to be
They were from an Orangutan steeped in a cup of tea

For several months then buried in the ground
Near the little town of Piltdown where other bones were found

So we are no nearer to finding the missing link
To be a fossil hunter is harder than you think

It's rare to find a fossil that is complete and true
Normally a fossil holds just a clue or two

This tale that I'm about to tell written for you by me
Is my view of this verdant isle and its history

Not too serious nor too long I'll try not to be boring
I hope that you will read it before you are heard snoring

What really happened long ago may not be as we think
There was nothing written no paper pen or ink

The question that I asked myself was easy enough to say
Who was the first King of this land we now call UK

King Alfred he who burned the cakes was the first to claim
That he was King of Angleland and Wessex his domain

King Arthur whence from Camelot a Kingdom of great mystery
With Guinevere his lovely queen they claimed their place in history

There was Merlin the Magician and the Knights of the round table
Did they really live and love or were they mostly fable

Aardvark

Did you know the Aardvark in the daytime can be found
Sleeping in his burrow underneath the ground

Where it is much cooler down there in the shade
Dreaming about termites washed down with lemonade

He's a funny looking fellow with a snout a bit like a pig
And claws like little shovels you should see him dig

He only lives in Africa where there's termites to be had
If you get one in your garden he will drive you nearly mad

Some folk have tried to eat them but because they just eat ants
They don't taste too special, in fact a pile of pants

They are not seen on the menu and unless I am mistaken
You'll never see a Dutchman eating eggs and Aardvark bacon

So what's so good about Aardvarks if you keep one in a pen
He'll dig his way out overnight and not be seen again

But if you see the phonebook on the very first page you'll find
That Aardvarks are in business and trade of every kind

There's Aardvark central heating and Aardvark builders who
Fit solar panels central heating and double glazing too

Not a Warthog nor a Hippo not a Rhino nor Gnu
If you really want their number you'll have to ask the zoo

Stone Age

This is the tale of who or what why and sometimes how
From long before our times began until how it is right now

From information mythical on paper never written
This is now what we believe was going on in Britain

About 4000 years ago metal not invented
The people lived upon the land apparently contented

It seems that there was room for all to live upon the land
With nothing more than what came readily to hand

All they had was what they made they gathered sticks and stones
Animal skins for winter warmth their needles made from bones

They could plan no further than the next hot meal
Not enough to fight for nothing there to steal

There was no need to have a king to sit upon a throne
And ponder why Stonehenge was built by persons unbeknown

They wandered freely where they wished there was no need to settle
Till they noticed in the fire that certain stones gave metal

The alchemists had heard reports a mix of fact and fable
That from these rare and special stones they soon would be able

To melt the metal we call copper and another we call tin
Let them melt together they make quite a different thing

This new metal they called bronze was very light and strong
It must be good for something it didn't take them long

Cutlery and drinking cups tools to work the land
Molten metal poured to set in moulds made in the sand

The Sea Bed

At the bottom of the sea
What a dreadful place to be

Cold as ice and dark as night
Creatures down there can they bite

There's not much choice about what to eat
Never heard of eggs or meat

Vegetables are just a wish
Mostly they get fish and fish

Yes that's right if fish eat fish
Then while eating one another

They might eat a fish they know
Or eat their baby brother

So it's a funny way of life
Down there on the seabed

No such thing as fish and wife
No time or place to get wed

A female fish lays lots of eggs
She lays them in the sea

To be exposed to wind and tide
What will be will be

These tiny fishes oh so small
Grow up fast and fecund

They must taste good to bigger fish
Who eat them by the thousand

Those who survive the first few months
Their survival instincts strongest

Have learned that in this cold place
He who eats first lives longest

That is the way they live
Down on the ocean floor

Where just a few fish live today
There were once many more

So where have all the fishes gone
That used to be so easy

To catch and cook as fish and chips
From the sea so clear and breezy

Well fishermen have taken most
In nets too small by miles

Big boats small mesh
Fishermen all smiles

No fish shops with a marble slab
Selling fish fresh from the sea

Your fish is in the freezer
Ready battered for your tea

The fish you buy there is not so good
But will do you no harm

Like cows and sheep upon the land
Fish too comes from a farm

Turbot Bass and Salmon
Fish that used to be

Sold as prime and of the
Very highest quality

But these fish upon your plate
Are not quite what you see

They may look and taste alright
But they have not been free

A King without a Kingdom

Way back then when boys were men
There was no rule of law

If might was right a man would fight
If he liked not what he saw

If he was rough and tough enough
And only fought to win

He would be the last man standing
And he would be king

A Chronicle of Kings and Queens

A Chronicle of Kings and Queens
Or should I say those ruling

Who was on the throne and when
Our history was our schooling

Not many of us can recall
The details of our monarchs

Is it that important now
Or just a load of rubbish

This is my book of answers
To questions of the past

So when at the next quiz night
Someone else comes last

The only date we know for sure
Is what we call AD

Since that date the birth of Christ
We have a history

Iron Age

One day a smelter to his mate said
You know I reckon

With a handle and an edge this would make
A damn good weapon

The smelter then discovered
With a new found ore

The blades he made were sharper
Than anything before

Good for swords and good for knives good for shields and axes
With horses and some men well-armed you could collect the taxes

Wealth and power they were seized but only by the tough
The greedy took the lions share but that was not enough

Invaders came from overseas, they wanted even more
Killed those who resisted and took the spoils of war

The people of this pleasant isle a land but not a nation
Fled to forests and to hills when news came of invasion

The strong ruled with a fist of iron the weaker were abused
Pay homage to your new crowned king or die if you refused

The reason for this rhyming tale is to help those who like me
Had more important things to do than study history

But I decided long ago that I had been a busy fool
I should have listened closer in my history class at school

So before it is too late and I am history myself
I've blown the dust off many books after too long on the shelf

This is my understanding of famous folk and things
Who they were and what they did - a chronicle of Kings
But these rulers not all men the women they fought too
Boudicca in her chariot killed more than just a few

So to be PC we can't assume that they were all patriarchs
Due deference must now be observed so I will call them monarchs

The Vikings

The Vikings were Norsemen rapacious and wild
Cared not who they killed man woman or child

A vile avaricious and murderous lot
They pillaged and burned took all we had got

The Britons by now had formed a disliking
Of the red bearded men from the north called the Vikings

There were plenty of Britons ready to fight
The Vikings outnumbered would surely take flight

But they needed a warrior to take the top job
A wise man a ruler not a murderous yob

Sagacious and fearless he had to be strong
If he wasn't the strongest he wouldn't last long

He would need a new army to see off the hoards
And show them no mercy if they drew their swords

When times were more peaceful a kingdom was small
But times were a changing the winner took all

The average King was ready to fight
But to be a great King you had to be bright

If you're King you'll need a kingdom of course
Unless you are a prince you must take one by force

That happened in Europe nigh a millennium past
Our throne became vacant and the Danes they moved fast

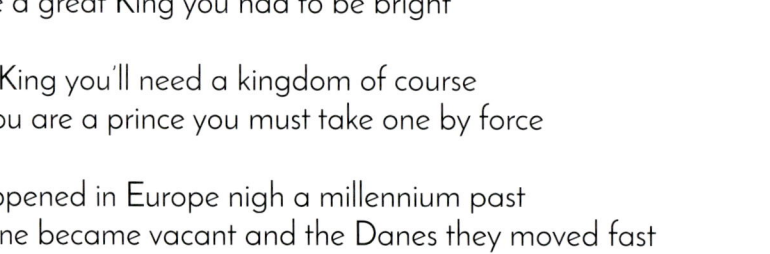

They lived very close just over the water
Liked nothing more than pillage and slaughter

While the locals got angry and their fate did bemoan
Forkbeard from Denmark he seized the throne

Till a battle was lost and Forkbeard was slain
His son was in Norway said he would reign

King Canute

The new King from Norway to England he came
He was a good King but he had a strange name

There were a few battles to confirm the decision
Who would wear the crown with no more derision

But the people of England said no that they could
Never pay homage to a King called Knud

But Knud was a King and very astute
He would choose his own name he would be King Canute

Not King Canute he's a fool you may shout
He sat on the beach told the tide to go out

If you think that Canute was not very strong
You think again as you have it wrong

Even worse if you think he wasn't so bright
Then you are the fool the King was alright

The fawning sycophants with whom he made court
Thought that with flattery the King could be bought

But Canute was smarter than them by a mile
He accepted their praise and returned a feint smile

Usurpers and traitors claimed that the new King
Had magical powers could do anything

They said they were certain that if he tried
He could command that the sea could miss a high tide

The King being modest as well as restrained
Reminded his subjects that he had never claimed

To have any power to influence affairs
To the detriment of others least of all theirs

The failure to stem the flood of the tide
Clear to be seen too clear to hide

Was proof that the traitors were up to no good
They incurred the displeasure of good King Knud

Diminutive Denizens

These little gems with names so charming
Have a beauty quite disarming

Lady Pyramid and Bee
Grow near here for all to see

Monkey Spider Green Winged too
Little beauties there for you

Early Purple Man and Fly
Eyes wide open lest you pass by

March Heath and Lizard rare
There to see if you know where

Bird's-nest Burnt Tip Cephalanthera
Helliborine long remembered if once seen

The Musk is small and seldom seen
It's very small and very green

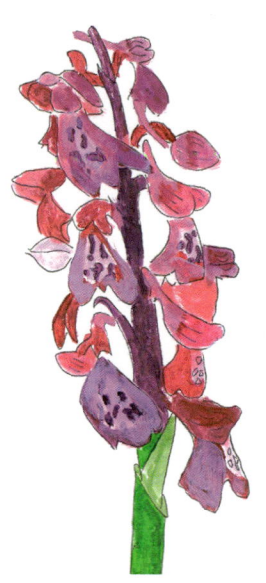

Twayblade green like the frog
Of which a few grow in a bog

Fragrant Pink Butterfly white
Complete the list well not quite

Not last nor least the Spotted Common
Has no name to be forgotten

Red or White can both be seen
Must be Epipactis helliborine

The Military or Soldier can be found
At a place with wire fences round

But where the Ladies Slipper grows
Could be found but no-one knows

Just where to look and feast one's eyes
Would be the ultimate surprise

To find one growing free and wild
Would leave you permanently beguiled

A Land Down Under

An island in the ocean the largest ever seen
In fact it was a continent where Europeans had never been

Till found in 1770 by Capt Cook the sailor
Who claimed it for the English and named the land Australia

The local population didn't like him when they met
Their descendants in no hurry have not warmed to us just yet

They found unusual creatures when they first settled there
Some were cute and cuddly like the koala bear

Who lives in the high branches of the eucalyptus tree
And eats only eucalyptus leaves for breakfast dinner and tea

If you are in Queensland and you see a toothy smile
You could be in big trouble with a sea going crocodile

The biggest reptile in the world would eat you as a snack
If you ever see one run like hell and don't look back

Kangaroos and wallabies if only they could talk
Might tell us why it is that they choose not to walk

They seem to have decided that the way to get around
Is a skippity hoppity leaping kind of bound

The hardest way to get around they set a cracking pace
And would bounce their way to victory if there was a race

Another bunch of creatures warm blooded just like us
The strangest in the whole wide world the duck billed platypus

They have beaks but are not birds they swim but cannot fly
Their prehistoric relatives have gone but these guys just won't die

When they are out of water you can see they have four legs
But even more surprising is their burrow nest and eggs

A final word of warning before you use the Aussi loo
There may be another creature there with his eye on you

You will not see this stranger waiting for you to come
Who when you have your trousers down will bite you in the bum

This nasty little arachnid lurking neath your rim
Looks like he is trouble and his bite is grim

The Wedding Speech

Why is it that we don't have a word
That in polite company will ever be heard

To describe that stuff that gets up your nose
And refuses to move no matter how hard you blows

Way up your nose it continues to linger
Heaven forbid you should use a finger

You need to be certain it just wouldn't do
I won't be a minute just off to the loo

Back to the wedding and the people you know
Twitching and wiggling your nose as you go

You rise to speak but go weak at the knees
Something has happened you can breathe now with ease

 One thing is certain there can be no doubt
If it's not up your nose it must have dropped out

You scratch your top lip it seems to be clean
Your chin smooth shaven nothing there to be seen

But what was that in the corner of my eye
Something dark on my cheek but up very high

I touch my cheek nonchalantly not there any more
If it's not on the table must be on the floor

The wedding is over the guests say goodbye
Not one of them mentioned the stuff near my eye

So back to my car and what do I see
In the rear view mirror as I turn the key

Is it that stuff to mention I dare not
Could it be I wonder no it's not no it's snot

A Frog on a Bus

The frog wished that he had caught the bus
But the driver didn't stop
We don't carry frogs no more
He shouted you will have to hop

The last time he had caught a bus
A lady with blue hair
Cried what does he think he's doing
He hasn't paid his fare

The frog he was offended
Didn't think that it was funny
How could he pay the fare
He didn't have any money

Frogs live in ponds most of the year
And are always wet
They can't get clothes with pockets
At least not dry ones yet

So till they get a currency
Perhaps the floating pound
Frogs will have a problem
How to get around

A Snail's Travail

I met a slug the other day
On the road to Dover
He was hoping a truck might stop
And give him a lift over

He told me that he knew a snail
Who went to France to see
If they really do eat snails
In garlic butter for their tea

He was worried about the snail
Who said he'd keep in touch
He had only had one post card
It wasn't very much

So he set off to France to help
His little friend the snail
Who might be in some trouble
Or even a French jail

He had tried almost everywhere
But no one seemed to know
Where he could find a restaurant
That served les escargots

So he slipped into a restaurant
Where a snail he knew
Said that he might find them
On the gastronome menu

He found them on the menu
And much to his surprise
There were some other things there
He could not believe his eyes

He knew the French enjoyed their food
And ate some things that we
Would never think of eating
Such as cuisses des grenouilles

But on the plat du jour
Served with a brandy sauce
The faux filet looked quite delicious
But it was not beef but horse

So beware of hungry Frenchmen
Who given half a chance
Will try to eat just anything
That grows or lives in France

In the Doctor's Waiting Room

In the doctor's waiting room
With a dozen more I sit

There's not much wrong with them I think
They all look pretty fit

Aches and pains runny noses
Need prescriptions I supposes

Grazes cuts and nasty bruises
Seasick pills for those on cruises

Nothing wrong with me I say just have to get a chit
From the Doctor to confirm that paradise admit

A healthy bloke from the British Isles who doesn't want to stay
More than a fortnight yes that's right just for a holiday

River Blindness sleeping sickness
I don't think that I've had either

I remember as I kid
My mum said I had a fever

Caught anything from any one who has been abroad
I never heard the like of it whatever next good lord

Beriberi let me think I remember feeling queer
On a day trip once to Calais I came home with diarrhoea

I never had a day off sick in 40 years or more
At this rate we'll be here all day just to make quite sure

What about malaria from a mosquito bite
If you are fit and strong you'll pull through all right

Have you ever been to any place marked upon this map
In red to indicate that you should see the chap

Who'll give you a little permit in your pocket you must keep
This is getting past a joke enough to make you weep

That will be two hundred pounds you can pay by credit card
How much I muttered beneath my breath I tried so very hard

Not to seem ungrateful nor angry about the price
The place that we are going to is really not that nice

So I said I just remembered a foreign fellow who had lots
And lots of nasty looking itchy weepy spots

I didn't know him Doctor whence he cometh nor his name
But to be on the safe side we will cancel just the same

We'll stay in good old England at a guest house by the sea
Have fish and chips in paper and a cuppa tea

No need to worry about those foreign things untold
The worst thing that we can catch at home is the common cold

Cockroach

I may be just a cockroach but I wonder why
People give me things to eat that will surely make me die

Perhaps I am too quick for them to crush beneath their feet
And that is the reason why they give me poison things to eat

I asked my friend the beetle if they tried to kill him too
He said that someone once hit his father with a shoe

The beetle also told me that he had seen that very day
A new and strong insecticide in a handy spray

With a special additive designed to kill us quick
Even just a little sniff will make you pretty sick

Now we don't think that we deserve to die because we eat
Some food put out for us that looks and smells so sweet

Mother Nature had her reasons and was probably quite right
That we insects have for rotting food a healthy appetite

Without us there to eat the food that others leave to rot
The world would be a smellier place if mistaken I am not

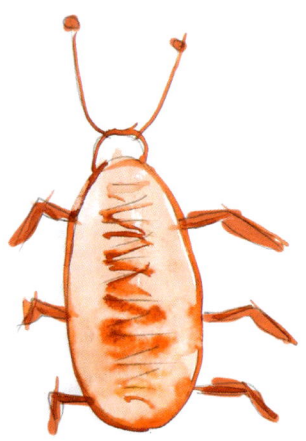

A Bunch of Thyme

A sneer of butlers seems to sum them up just right
A parliament of owls held a meeting in the night

Corgis come in consorts and travel with the Queen
While a diffidence of debutants is hardly ever seen

An armoury of aardvarks will get underneath the wire
A conflagration of arsonists will set the place on fire

A boast of suited barristers and a troupe of dancers
Had to do a quickstep because they had no answers

An eloquence of lawyers offered a fistful of pounds
For a lock of golden hair and a couple and a half of hounds

A bench of judges sat on a clutch of eggs and made a wish
For a parcel of fat hogs and a kettle of fresh fish

A savoir faire of frenchmen had caught and put in boxes
While they wondered how to cook a skulk of rabid foxes

An erudition of editors knew not what to do
When a curse of angry creditors took a bus to London Zoo

A skein of geese flew honking like a clarion of bells
A loquacity of barbers met a giggle of teenage girls

A hand of cards was dealt by a bishop in a mitre hat
A coven of wrinkled witches said to the cat see that

Redit Redit Hopit Plop

A frog sat by a muddy pond
He thought it would be cool

To lounge upon a sun bed
Beside a swimming pool

He had seen them having fun
Beside the pool next door

He would love to be there with them
No frog could ask for more

He figured he could use their pool
If he knew they were all out

The frog was so excited
If he had a voice he'd shout

Come with me I know a place
Where we can have some fun

But the frog he had no voice
To call to anyone

One day the frog was all alone
The pool looked so exciting

He never thought that for his life
He would so soon be fighting

In his haste to take the plunge
He forgot to think about

The ease with which he could jump in
And how he could get out

The frog was happy
In the pool till it occurred to him

With no help and no way out
He had to sink or swim

The frog he was not worried
As he swam round and round

He never thought he'd be remembered
As the frog that drowned

He swam and swam the sun went down
And daylight turned to night

The frog he was an optimist
He thought he'd be alright

It was after midnight he was cold
And feeling really groggy

Too cold to swim another stroke
Was this the end for froggy

The light of dawn was slow to grow
But the sun at last was risen

The frog was floating
Only just in his watery prison

It was a lovely morning
The wealthy fellow was about

He saw the frog still floating
And with a net he fished him out

The sun was shining brighter now
Where he had been thrown

Bringing vital warmth
To the old cold paving stone

With the warm sun on his back
He was feeling much stronger

He decided it was time to go
He should stay no longer

Back to his muddy pond he hopped
Where would he choose to rest

Among the yellow Irises
He thought would be the best

He had forgotten as frogs do
It was a bad mistake

The yellow Irises were the home
Of a long and hungry snake

Who thought the frog though slimy
Looked good enough to eat

Was this a gift from heaven
Would this be easy meat

So thought the snake as he slithered up
Behind the frog who looked so tasty

He had been told by other snakes
Not to be too hasty

Now the frog was bigger than the snake
Who failed to realise

You simply cannot swallow
Something more than twice your size

The snake decided that the frog
Would make a splendid meal

He would worry when the time came
About how he might feel

He decided he should eat the frog
His hunger to allay

No time like the present
No need to delay

If you think the frog was stupid
The snake must have been barmy

He tried to eat in one great feast
Enough to feed an army

He had a pile of trouble
But to make things even worse

The silly snake decided
To eat just one leg first

But the snake had second thoughts
He realised there was no way

That he could eat a frog so big
And live to rue the day

So with a lot of wriggling and
Writhing on the ground

The snake coughed up the poor old frog
Who didn't hang around

He saw the way was open
A chance to make a break

The Frog made an almighty hop
He made a brave escape

So here we have the story of the
Greedy hungry snake

Who tried to eat a frog so big
It gave him tummy ache

He had learned a lesson
That we all have to too

Not to be so greedy
And bite off more than we can chew

The frog he learned his lesson
And was lucky to survive

To look before you leap
Will help you stay alive

These simple rules that show us
How and when and where

Are the wisdom of our forebears
Passed on for us to share

The Man in the Mirror

The man in the mirror
He used to be me

I knew where to find him
I knew where he'd be

But the man in the mirror
Was no longer me

Just an imposter who thought he could be
There in my place where I ought to be

And to tell me the truth about who I might see
I always thought that he could see me

There in the mirror apparently free
But it seems that the man who I thought was me

And made my decisions about who I should be
Was no longer free to choose who he would be

He was who he is not free to be me

If the man in the mirror used to be me
Then who was I and who did I see here in the mirror

He was who he is not free to be me
Looking back at me reminding me who I once used to be

And how I might look if I too was free
To be a man in a mirror for someone like me

Pigs

My dog will do all that I ask and be my friend for ever
My cat won't even look my way no tricks today or ever

My silly sheep does nowt but bleat for her little lamb so pretty
Who'll soon be on a butchers hook at the market in the city

My chickens ducks and turkeys all birds of a feather
Don't have three penneth twixtem if you put them all together

But my pig he really likes me I can see it in his eye
When I stop and have a chat with him if I see him in his sty

A pig sty has no luxuries and they must make do
It may have got good neighbours but it doesn't have a loo

So the pig who is by nature a tidy sort of chap has nowhere to go
when nature calls and he needs a loo

So his place is in a mess it's really quite a pity
That pigs must pooh upon the floor and leave it rather messy

Another thing regarding pigs that doesn't seem quite fair
Is that a pig don't have no fur just a few stiff hairs

So at a glance a pig appears well terribly rude
Without no fur and being pink he looks like he is nude

But he is cool cares not who sees his curly tail so pink
And doesn't know what people mean when they say he stinks

So all in all the pig has got a shabby reputation
As happy as a pig in pooh must be a misquotation

The Romans

We saw their ships as they left France.
We saw them coming over

These guys were looking for a fight
Not a shopping trip to Dover

They landed on the beach at Deal a terrifying sight
Not a Briton to be seen too many for a fight

It was raining when they landed still raining the next day
Patiently they waited but it didn't go away

Said Caesar to his troops so wet what are we doing here
Let us go home for Christmas and come again next year

I came I saw I conquered said the emperor of Rome
Give us just a year or two we'll have this place like home

In a letter to the senate he told of this verdant isle
Ready to be conquered and Roman for a while

They stayed about 400 years and taught us many ways
Pizza Lamborghini and Spaghetti bolognaise

The Bastard Duke

The sea now called the English Channel wasn't all that wide
From the cliff tops now called Dover you could see the other side

Invaders came and plundered, took all that they could find
There wasn't much to take even less was left behind

Angles Saxons Jutes and Vikings Celts and Britons too
Some Romans and some French to name all but a few

These were the folk that lived here had been here many a year
They lived in their own regions their boundaries not quite clear

There were many Kingdoms and castles throughout the land
Kings and Queens fought battles they tried to make a stand

To make this land a monarchy and have a king upon a throne
To lead them from the Iron Age to make this land their own

But not so very far away just below the horizon out of sight
The Bastard Duke of Normandy was gathering his might

1066 was the year Hastings was the place
William the aggressor would Harold show his face

Edward the confessor had been king without an heir
A drop of blood from King Canute helped Harold to the chair

Before the Duke seized power the Anglo Saxons were in charge
They claimed the south of England their domain was not that large

But the north was run by Celts who didn't give a toss
Who they killed or injured to show just who was boss

The Bastard Duke of Normandy was born to a tanner's daughter
He liked the look of England just across the water

The regions we call Scotland and England today
Had borders that hitherto were just too far away

But William the Bastard was not easily dissuaded
With promises of lands and riches his army soon invaded

The Duke he crossed the channel to storm the British coast
Hastings was the landing place that he fancied most

The battle raged in Battle the arrows did they fly
His shield dropped for a moment Harold took one in his eye

With their leader mortally wounded the will to fight was lost
Harold died in battle the Anglo Saxons paid the cost

The Duke had many friends in France all looking for a break
Just a few thousand acres with forest and a lake

But this was strictly business come do and have a look
If you want to call it yours sign in the Doomsday Book

The Duke soon moved to London to sit upon his throne
To collect his dues and taxes and hear the Barons groan

He brought in laws throughout the land that taxes should be paid
In accordance with the laws that William had just made

To take a rabbit from the forest the property of the King
Punished by death sentence the poacher he did swing

At Sea

Nothing stood still for the coldness to root
No frost ever seen on the ocean
The wind drove the waves till its strength was consumed
Salt water in perpetual motion

The horizon cut sharp like a filleting knife
The scent of the sea on the nose
There's nowhere on earth they would rather be
Than at sea where the fisherman goes

Like a mirror laid flat reflecting the blue
The sea all around us grew calm
The water was clear our target was near
May god give strength to our arms

The sound of exhaust discharged under water
A gurgling burbling splutter
Unique to a diesel at work on the sea
A reassuring mechanical mutter

Ready to fish expectation is high
The wind stays in the north and falls lighter
The motor slows down to a leisurely pace
Action follows the mood becomes brighter

Fish on the deck too many to count
Our boxes all full spilling over
The gathering wind unnoticed till now
Will we be wet before we reach Dover

Frog Up

The frog he had forgotten that just the day before
He had very nearly drowned in the pool next door
Yet here he was ready for more before he was quite dry
Looking up and wondering if he could learn to fly

He watched the birds take to the air
It seemed to him to be unfair
That birds could fly with such ease
And stop to sing high in the trees

Now the frog he was determined that he should get some wings
And fly like other fliers such as butterflies and things
He always thought that flying was the way to see
And that there was no reason why the pilot should not be he

But the frog he had no money to buy an aeroplane
To get him up into the air and safely down again
So he went to the airport to see a pilot who could teach
Him how to fly to places he thought he'd never reach

Well my lad the pilot said with a chuckle when he saw
Not sure if it will ever fly it's been there since the war
But as I don't have much else to do said the pilot with a snigger
And we have some pots of paint somewhere this project is getting
  bigger

The frog he took a hop around to see his family in the pond
And tell them of his latest project you will need a magic wand
They laughed until they cried then they laughed some more
The frog he was offended as they rolled upon the floor

The frog he needed something to improve his self esteem
A journey somewhere dangerous where frogs are seldom seen
By an oasis in the desert where nothing ever grew
Why he chose to go there no-one ever knew

He could not get there easily it was just too frogging far
He tried to ride his camel he crashed his motor car
But he was a tough old frog and would not be beaten
If anything got in his way chances were it would be eaten

So the frog decided that he had to become well known
And hop his way to freedom from this land of sand and stone
It was a mighty journey for a tiny little frog
Who you would not expect to find more than a short hop from a bog

Well the frog he made it with blisters on his feet
The crowd turned out to welcome him and mark his froggy feat
The frog he got a heroes welcome from all for miles around
The welcome still can be heard when the frog he is in town